THE BUMPY LITTLE PUMPKIN

BY Margery Cuyler
ILLUSTRATED BY Will Hillenbrand

SCHOLASTIC INC.
New York Toronto London Auckland Sydney
Mexico City New Delhi Hong Kong Buenos Aires

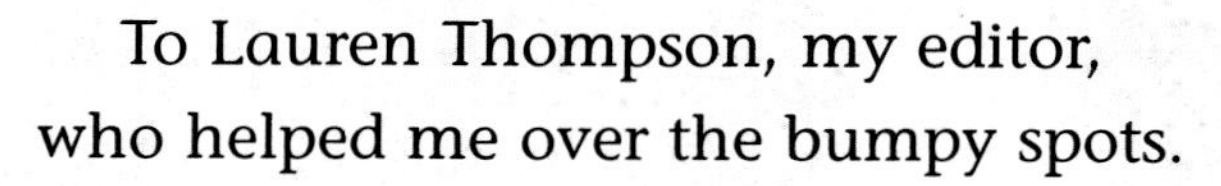

To Lauren Thompson, my editor,
who helped me over the bumpy spots.

—M. C.

To Brennan, little but mighty! And to Argi, who loves jack-o'-lanterns
as much as I do.

With a very special thanks to Lauren: I couldn't have done this without you!

And to Margery ... thanks for bringing Nell back.

—W. H.

ISBN 0-439-78890-0

12 11 10 9 8 7 6 5 4 3 2 1 5 6 7 8 9 10/0

Printed in the U.S.A. 40

First Scholastic paperback printing, September 2005

The text type was set in 14-point Stone Informal.
The illustrations were created on vellum using oils, egg tempera, watercolors, water-soluble artist crayons, and pencil, as well as collage.
Book design by Kristina Albertson

Little Nell lived with BIG Mama, BIG Sarah, and BIG Lizzie in a great, BIG house in a great, BIG woods.

Behind the great, BIG house, there was a great, BIG garden, and in the great, BIG garden, there was a great, BIG pumpkin patch.

All summer long, Little Nell had helped her family water and weed so that the pumpkins would grow BIG and orange for Halloween.

When Halloween finally came, BIG Mama called Little Nell and her sisters into the kitchen.

"It's time for each of you to pick a pumpkin to carve!" she said in her BIG, blustery voice.

"Me too?" asked Little Nell.

"You too," said BIG Mama.

So Little Nell followed her sisters out to the pumpkin patch.

"There are so many wonderful pumpkins, it's hard to choose," said BIG Sarah. She picked up a tall, skinny pumpkin. "I think I like this one," she said.

BIG Lizzie picked up a round, fat pumpkin. "This is the one for me!"

But Little Nell couldn't decide. She walked back and forth, back and forth, back and forth, looking at all the pumpkins. Some were big, some were small, some were crooked, some were tall, but none was just right.

At last she came to the end of the patch, and there sat a bumpy, little pumpkin all by itself.

"This one's my favorite," said Little Nell.

"It's bumpy and little and ugly," said BIG Lizzie.

"It could have a nice, smiley face," said Little Nell.

"No way," said BIG Sarah. "How about this nice, smooth one instead?"

"I like the bumpy one," said Little Nell.

BIG Sarah and BIG Lizzie rolled their eyes.

"We're taking our pumpkins inside," said BIG Sarah.

"You keep looking till you find a bigger and better one," said BIG Lizzie.

"Then we'll help you carve it," added BIG Sarah.

After they left, Little Nell sat down next to the bumpy, little pumpkin. A tiny tear fell down her cheek, then another and another.

Her friends Reindeer, Hare, and Bear Cub came along.

"What's wrong?" asked Bear Cub.

Little Nell sniffled and snuffled. "BIG Lizzie and BIG Sarah think my pumpkin's too bumpy and too little and too ugly to make a good jack-o'-lantern."

"I don't think it's too bumpy," said Bear Cub.

"Or too little," said Reindeer.

"Or too ugly," said Hare.

"You don't?" asked Little Nell.

"No!" said the animals.

“This pumpkin would make a great jack-o’-lantern,” said Reindeer. “And we could help you carve it.”

“How?” asked Little Nell.

“Like this,” said Reindeer. He lowered his head and cut around and around and around the top until he’d carved a lid.

“Oooh!” said Little Nell. “That’s perfect.”

"I can scoop out the insides," said Bear Cub.

"How?" asked Little Nell.

"Like this," said Bear Cub. He clawed and pawed and pawed and clawed until there was nothing left but an empty pumpkin shell.

"Oh, goody," said Little Nell. "Now for the face. How can we do that?"

"Let's ask the birds to help," said Hare.

So Little Nell whistled for the birds. Crow, Cardinal, and Sparrow flew down from the trees.

"Could you make the face for my jack-o'-lantern?" asked Little Nell.

"What kind of face?" asked Cardinal.

With her finger, Little Nell etched and sketched and sketched and etched a face in the dirt. It had triangles for eyes, a square for a nose, and a smiley, lopsided mouth.

"Like this," she said.

So Crow, Cardinal, and Sparrow poked and pecked and pecked and poked until the pumpkin had a face.

At last, the jack-o'-lantern was finished.

Little Nell smiled a tiny smile. "I can't wait to show it to BIG Mama, BIG Sarah, and BIG Lizzie."

She picked it up and ran
all the way to the house.

"What a beautiful jack-o'-lantern!" said BIG Mama. "Where did you get it?"

"From our pumpkin patch," said Little Nell.

"But who helped you carve it?" asked BIG Sarah.

"My friends Reindeer, Bear Cub, and Hare," said Little Nell.

"I still think it's little and bumpy and ugly!" said BIG Lizzie.

"Nonsense," said BIG Mama. "Jack-o'-lanterns come in all shapes and sizes!"

BOO

The girls placed their jack-o'-lanterns near the door, and BIG Mama lit them.

"Mine's cool," said BIG Sarah.

"Mine's even cooler," said BIG Lizzie.

"They're *all* wonderful," said BIG Mama.

"Even mine?" asked Little Nell.

"Even yours," said BIG Mama, and she leaned over and gave Little Nell a BIG, sloppy kiss.

Little Nell smiled.

HAPPY HALLOWEEN!